romero and juliette

dog tags

book seven

Kat Baxter

Romero and Juliette

Kat Baxter

Edited by: Emily Beierle-McKaskle

Copyeditor: Geeky Girl Author Services

Book cover: Cormar Covers

Cover image: Jane Ashley Converse Photography and Images

Cover model: Jordan Wheeler

romero and juliette

CRUZ

I swore I was done with surprises.

Then I found a stowaway in my van—a too-young, too-tempting mechanic who's supposed to be fixing engines, not wrecking my focus. Juliette Winslow is everything good and sweet wrapped in grease-stained overalls, and she's got no idea the guy she's been flirting with on a dating app is me.

Now we're stuck together on a road trip, sharing bad coffee, cramped motel rooms, and way too much tension. I'm old enough to know better. But when she smiles at me like that? Better goes straight out the window.

Juliette

Maybe sneaking into Cruz Romero's van wasn't my best idea.

But if I waited around for permission, I'd never live a little—or find love. I thought my crush was a blip, but the stoic ex-Ranger with a decade and change on me—makes me forget every reason he should be off-limits. He's the kind of man who fixes what's broken. The kind of man I could fall for—hard.

But Cruz has secrets, and one of them might just break my heart. Because somewhere between pit stops and puppy rescues, I'm realizing the man behind the screen might be sitting right next to me.

chapter **one**

JULIETTE

Online dating is not for the weak-minded. Or the weak-stomached, for that matter. I finally found an app that doesn't unlock pictures until you go through several stages of communication. It can be frustrating, but it's eliminated the dick pics, which I appreciate.

You would think that working as a mechanic at my family's garage would mean I have loads of opportunities to meet guys. And I guess I do, in some ways. But the truth is, I've lived in Saddle Creek, Texas, my entire life, and most of the guys around here have been here the whole time.

I wouldn't call myself an adventurous person, but I am interested in people who didn't grow up here. I want to meet someone who has life experience that looks different from mine. Small-town Texas is a wonderful place to live. I don't even think I want to move away or anything, I just want to know someone different.

Kinda like my brother, Jude, and my sister-in-law, Emory. Technically, she's a small-town girl too, but she traveled all over before she ended up here. She has some of the best stories from when she was on the road all the time.

In any case, I started this online dating journey a few months ago and it has been interesting and eye-opening, to say the least. But no real connections yet. I haven't told anyone in my family about this venture. They'll tell me I'm too young to be looking for my forever.

Age is irrelevant. I'm a legal adult, that's all that matters. I'm old enough to do pretty much whatever I want. Except for renting a car, but I don't have any need to do that, so I'm good.

But the raw truth of it all is that no one is guaranteed a nice, long life. My family should understand that more than most. Our parents died in an accident when I was seven. Jude was barely twenty, but he put his entire life on hold for me, Aria, and Sofia. So we'd all stay together and not get put into foster care. I know it was a massive sacrifice.

I don't remember a lot about my parents since they've been gone so long, but I do know they were wildly in love with each other. They planned to grow old together, but that didn't happen. So yeah, no one is guaranteed anything.

If I don't get to live a long life, I at least want to live one next to someone I'm wildly in love with. Thus, the online dating.

Randall#1: You're gorgeous. Like, I can't stop staring at your pics.

FleetwdLvr05: My pics don't have any with my face.

Randall#1: But you're curves are banging.

FleetwdLvr05: Uh… thanks.

Randall#1: Seriously, I think you might be my dream girl.

FleetwdLvr05: ...That's a lot for a Tuesday.

. . .

And Randall#1 gets blocked.

FleetwdLvr05: Hey! How's your week going?

Ryan89: Hey. Busy. You?

FleetwdLvr05: Same. Trying to survive on coffee and good intentions.

Ryan89: Lol same here.

I exit the chat. I won't block him because maybe he's just busy. But sheesh, learn how to have a back-and-forth conversation.

FleetwdLvr05: Hey, what kind of music do you like?

Fit4Life: Whatever you dance to, gorgeous. 😏

FleetwdLvr05: Uh... okay, but seriously, favorite band?

Fit4Life: Anything fast with a groove so I can get my dance on. When are we grabbing drinks?

FleetwdLvr05: ...I think I'm busy forever.

Who talks like that? Moving on.

Mustang_Ranger: Hey, I saw you mention sunshine, dogs and tacos in your profile. That's basically my holy trinity right there.

FleetwdLvr05: Haha, same. Add margaritas to the mix and we're soulmates.

Mustang_Ranger: Okay, but crucial question — crunchy or soft tacos? This could make or break us. 🌮😁

FleetwdLvr05: Soft. But only if the tortilla's warm. You?

Mustang_Ranger: Crunchy. I guess this is our first fight. We'll need to talk it out over margaritas.

Lame screen name, but promising as far as the conversation.

FleetwdLvr05: Your profile says you make "the best coffee in town." That's a bold claim.

Joshua_TX99: It's true. I've been banned from three cafes for stealing their customers. ☕

FleetwdLvr05: Ha! What's your secret?

Joshua_TX99: Can't reveal it until our second date. First, you have to survive my bad puns.

Okay, Joshua, you have some promise too. I mean, who doesn't love a good pun?

FleetwdLvr05: Okay, serious question. Pineapple on pizza: yes or no?

Mustang_Ranger: Absolutely not. That's a war crime.

FleetwdLvr05: Wrong answer. You just failed the vibe check.

Mustang_Ranger: I'll take the loss. But if you bring the pineapple, I'll bring the pizza.

FleetwdLvr05: Deal. You've got good negotiation skills.

Mustang_Ranger: Part of my job.

FleetwdLvr05: Oh? What do you do?

Mustang_Ranger: A little bit of everything. Technically, I'm retired.

That's when I should ask him how old he is, but I truly don't care. I mean it's not like he's gonna be on this app if he's a grandfather or whatever.

Mustang_Ranger: What do you do besides eating blasphemous pizza and listening to a lot of Stevie Nicks?

He cracked my code. The code I didn't think was all that mysterious, but he's the first guy on here to recognize Fleetwood Mac. Hard not to find that attractive!

FleetwdLvr05: I work with my hands. Mostly engines.

Mustang_Ranger: A woman who knows how to get her hands dirty. Color me intrigued.

FleetwdLvr05: Rough day. I think my coffee machine hates me.

Mustang_Ranger: Coffee machines can sense weakness. You have to stare them down until they submit.

FleetwdLvr05: 😂 I tried that. It hissed at me.

Mustang_Ranger: Okay, maybe it's possessed. You want me to drop by with backup coffee?

FleetwdLvr05: Ha! You're not local, remember?

Mustang_Ranger: Right. But I'd still bring it if I could. Everyone deserves good coffee and a better day.

FleetwdLvr05: You're dangerously good at this, Ranger.

Mustang_Ranger: At what?

FleetwdLvr05: Making me smile.

chapter **two**

CRUZ

Everything started at that goddamn Bluebonnet Festival, back in the spring. I'd been minding my own business, sitting with my buddies at the beer tent and she'd walked by. It was the long blonde hair that had caught my attention at first, but then her luscious curves had locked in my gaze.

I'd nodded towards her and asked my friend, Dane, "Who's Princess Buttercup over there?"

He'd taken one look and had laughed.

When she'd finally turned around and I'd seen her face... well, that's when I knew I was so screwed. Sure, she was gorgeous, but the moment

I saw her face, I knew why Dane was laughing. Stunning or not, she was clearly way too young for the likes of me. Besides, there are too many beautiful women in the world for me to chase one who is too young to have a proper conversation with.

So I let it go, determined to forget about her.

Fate had other things in mind. And Saddle Creek is a small town. Two days later, I'm minding my own business when I pull up to the garage I bring my van to. I've been at that garage a lot over the last several months. The guys and I over at Great Dane's Dog Sanctuary needed a vehicle that could safely transport multiple dogs. So I've been working with Jude to outfit my van with built-in dog crates.

Most of our dogs come to us via delivery from other rescue organizations and shelters. But on occasion, I need to drive somewhere to pick some up. Usually, a roundup of pups on a shelter's euthanasia list or some dogs misplaced because of natural disasters. In Texas, that normally means floods or hurricanes.

Since the last thing I want is to end up stranded by the side of the road with a van full of traumatized pups, I bring my van by to get the all clear before each trip. And that's when things go from manageably bad to much worse.

I don't see Jude in the office, so I walk around the garage bays. There's music playing. Drift Away. And not the newer version by Uncle Kracker, but the original Dobie Gray version. There's a car with the hood up—a '65 Mustang Coupe. And there she is.

Buttercup.

And despite the nickname I gave her the first time I saw her, she doesn't look like a princess. She's wearing steel-toed work boots and a mechanic's coveralls, zipper open over a grime-streaked tank top. Her corn-silk blond hair is in a braid that wraps around her head. She's holding a torque wrench in her hand, and she's singing along with Dobie Gray as she sways with her eyes closed. There's a smear of motor oil on her cheek.

The fabric of her tank stretches tight as she raises one hand over her head to belt out the chorus.

And... I'm a goner.

Gone.

Lost.

Head over fucking heels.

This woman, whom I had every intention of never thinking about again, has become unforgettable.

Some nameless, gorgeous blonde chick at the festival I could have forgotten. Would have forgotten.

Saddle Creek is a tourist town, and people come in for those damn festivals all the time. By rights, I never should have seen Buttercup again.

But there she is, looking like a damn dream. A woman who works on cars, wears the proper foot protection, and belts out the lyrics of my favorite song?

You might as well stamp DOA on my forehead and ship my corpse home.

Yeah, that was like six months ago, and I swear things get worse every time I go. Last time I saw her, she was wearing an Eagles concert t-shirt. And not in the ironic way people wear thrift-store clothes. I've heard her sing their songs, too. So I'm a big dude who likes muscle cars and classic rock. I'm a cliché, whatever. It fits nicely with my pervy old-guy persona I've been developing.

Like I said, I'm completely fucked.

Which is why today, knowing I need to go to

the garage and have the van checked out before going on a run, I asked Flynn to come with me. Does that make me a pussy? Maybe, but it's always nice to have reinforcements.

We're currently sitting in the van a block away from the garage.

"The heart wants what the heart wants," Flynn says.

"What are you even talking about?" I ask, but I'm pretty sure I know.

"Juliette Winslow," he says.

"What about her?"

"I've seen the way you look at her. You have feelings."

"What? Happily married, and that somehow makes you a love guru? I'm having some pretty strong feelings about you right now."

Flynn chuckles.

"Well, it doesn't actually matter how I look at her, because the fact of it is, she's young enough to be my daughter."

"Is that how you think about her, like she's your daughter?"

"Fuck no. Not at all how I think about her, but I know how it would look. People would think I was a creepy old man."

"You're older than me, but that doesn't make you an old man," Flynn bumps my elbow. "Plenty of couples have significant age gaps. It's not a big deal. Besides, it's not like she's a child; she's an actual adult."

"Yeah, well, I'm pretty sure her brother would not see it that way, and he'd want to rearrange my face."

"Definitely a possibility. And Jude looks like he could be pretty mean, but you could probably kill him sixteen different ways, using just your pinky nail and a cotton swab."

I snort. "I don't think that's accurate." I turn into the parking lot of the garage. "I don't want to kill him. He's a good guy."

"Yep, he did a good job raising his sisters. Now they're all grown and they're going to fall in love with men and get married, and he's not going to be able to do anything about it, because, again, they're adults."

"Well, I don't want all three of them. I just want the one."

"Well, that's good considering that having multiple wives is still illegal in the state of Texas. I don't know how guys do that. I'll never want another woman the way I want my wife. Not only would Temple kill them, but she'd kick my ass, for sure."

"Wanting is not the same thing as deserving or attaining," I point out.

Flynn blows out a breath. "You're frustrating as fuck, my friend. How about we go about it from this angle? I've seen the way she looks at you."

"Oh, well, that is irrelevant. She isn't old enough to know what she wants."

"I'm calling bullshit! You don't even believe that."

"You're right. I don't. But still, none of this changes the fact that I'm way too damn old for her. She's too young and sweet, and she isn't old and cranky and jaded with a bad knee."

"That you know of. She might have a bad knee from an old football injury."

"You're an idiot, you know that?"

"You should have Temple teach you some yoga moves. You could probably loosen up that knee of yours."

"Yeah, I'll consider that. But in the meantime, I just need to get ready for this trip."

"You want me to go with you?"

"No, no, you stay here with your wife. I've

got it. It's not a big deal. It's not even that long of a drive, just about six hours each way. So it, it'll be good. I've got my tunes."

"I still think you should ask her out. "

"I hear your words, and I appreciate your opinions about my life, but I'm not going to ask her out. I'm fine. I don't need anybody."

"Well, that is a crock of shit. Everybody needs somebody."

"I don't. Some people were made to be alone. I'm one of those guys."

"Oh yeah, you're, what, the Lone Ranger?" Then he guffaws. "I didn't even mean to make that pun."

"You're a regular old comedian. Let's just drop it about Buttercup. I'm not asking her out. Besides, I'm kind of bonding with this chick on that dating app Evan signed me up for."

"The kid did that?"

"Yeah, about six months ago. I ignored it for months. But then decided to just see what it was about."

"I hope your username isn't The Lone Ranger."

"Fucker."

chapter three

CRUZ

The only thing that ever takes my mind off of Buttercup is my conversations with Fleetwood. Until now, dating apps haven't really been my thing. Sure, when I was younger, I'd use them for the rare, no-strings-attached hook-up. Because how the hell else is a single guy in special forces who's only state-side a couple of days at a time supposed to meet anyone?

Once I left the rangers, I tried a couple of the apps more suited to actual dating. It always felt flat. Forced.

Chatting with a stranger felt like a chore rather than something that might develop into a real relationship. Until Fleetwood. She's easy to talk to, even if we're not talking about anything real or meaningful. Everything with her feels effortless.

It's still hard to imagine it turning into an honest relationship when there's another woman taking up so much space in my mind, but I'm working on it. I like Fleetwood. It feels like the kind of friendship that could develop into something real if my fucking libido would get out of the way.

I started up the conversation because I needed someone to take my mind off Buttercup, but now, chatting with Fleetwood is the best part of my day.

FleetwdLvr05: You never said what you do for work.

Mustang_Ranger: I drive a lot.

FleetwdLvr05: Like Uber?

Mustang_Ranger: Something like that.

FleetwdLvr05: Mysterious and evasive. That's quite the combo.

Mustang_Ranger: Maybe I'm secretly a spy.

FleetwdLvr05: You'd have to be smoother for that.

Mustang_Ranger: You wound me.

FleetwdLvr05: You'll live, Ranger.

Mustang_Ranger: You say that like you care.

FleetwdLvr05: Maybe I do. Maybe I'm just being polite.

Mustang_Ranger: I don't think you're ever just polite.

FleetwdLvr05: You say that like you think you know me.

Mustang_Ranger: Nah. Just a feeling I have.

I do feel like I know her. Maybe that's crazy. But I've always been that way with people. The first time I met the guys on my team, we were one cohesive unit. Even being from different backgrounds, we meshed perfectly. I was part of several other units before where none of us worked well together. Like eating a corndog on fine china.

So yeah, I feel like I know Fleetwood.

Of course I feel like I know Buttercup too, but that is irrelevant.

FleetwdLvr05: How do you take your coffee?

Mustang_Ranger: You will judge me if I answer honestly.

FleetwdLvr05: Now I'm intrigued. Can I guess?

Mustang_Ranger: Go for it.

FleetwdLvr05: I'm guessing you're a latte kind of guy, but you're too embarrassed to order it out.

Mustang_Ranger: Well, you're partially correct. I am a latte guy, more flavor than coffee, but I need that caffeine.

FleetwdLvr05: So what part did I get wrong?

Mustang_Ranger: I'm man enough to order my coffee with extra whip, extra sweet, and with sprinkles on top.

FleetwdLvr05: LOL! I love that so much.

I dated a woman once who was so put off by how I drank my coffee that she ended things after our third date.

People are weird. And stupid.

But Fleetwood gets me. There's no judgment, only amusement. She just feels authentic in a way that most people don't even in person.

FleetwdLvr05: I just realized I've told you more than some people I've known for years.

Mustang_Ranger: That's the beauty of a screen. No pretending.

FleetwdLvr05: Or maybe we're both pretending really well.

Mustang_Ranger: You pretending with me?

FleetwdLvr05: Maybe a little. Maybe I like the mystery.

Mustang_Ranger: Careful. Mystery's addictive.

FleetwdLvr05: Guess I've already had a taste.

Am I pretending? No, I've been completely honest with her. That said, I can't help but be a little on guard. She comes across pretty damn amazing. Close to perfect. But when I'm messaging with her, my mind conjures images of Buttercup.

That's the problem.

I started chatting with her to forget about the pretty and way too young blonde that I seem to be infatuated with. But in some ways, it feels like Fleetwood has only made me want Buttercup more.

Which feels dishonest, somehow.

FleetwdLvr05: I bet you're the kind of guy who hates losing.

Mustang_Ranger: Depends on the game.

FleetwdLvr05: What if the prize is bragging rights?

Mustang_Ranger: I'd play hard.

FleetwdLvr05: And if the prize is a kiss?

Mustang_Ranger: Then I'd never lose.

FleetwdLvr05: That's cocky.

Mustang_Ranger: That's confidence. You'd like it.

FleetwdLvr05: Don't be so sure.

Mustang_Ranger: I'm sure enough to take the bet.

She is definitely flirting with me.

We're flirting.

And fuck me if I don't like it. Maybe she really is the one who can get Buttercup out of my head.

Mustang_Ranger: What's something small that always makes your day better?

FleetwdLvr05: Sunsets. Dogs. Good music.

Mustang_Ranger: Dogs, huh?

FleetwdLvr05: Yeah. I trust dogs more than people.

Mustang_Ranger: Smart girl.

FleetwdLvr05: What about you?

Mustang_Ranger: Quiet mornings. Fresh coffee. Someone who laughs easily.

FleetwdLvr05: Sounds nice.

Mustang_Ranger: It could be.

FleetwdLvr05: You saying you'd share it?

Mustang_Ranger: Depends who's asking.

FleetwdLvr05: Just some girl with pink boots.

What is it about this woman that makes me want to open up? To let her see all the parts of me? That feels like she wouldn't judge any of them?

FleetwdLvr05: Ever get that feeling like you know someone before you really do?

Mustang_Ranger: Yeah.

FleetwdLvr05: Like you recognize their energy or something.

Mustang_Ranger: Or maybe they just feel like home.

FleetwdLvr05: That's... unexpectedly poetic.

Mustang_Ranger: Don't tell anyone. It'll ruin my reputation.

FleetwdLvr05: Of being a mysterious cowboy spy?

Mustang_Ranger: Exactly.

FleetwdLvr05: Can't sleep. My brain won't shut off.

Mustang_Ranger: Try counting sheep.

FleetwdLvr05: Tried. The sheep started judging me.

Mustang_Ranger: You sure you weren't counting goats? They're bastards.

FleetwdLvr05: 😂 You sound like you've got experience.

Mustang_Ranger: I've met a few.

FleetwdLvr05: You ever have trouble sleeping?

Mustang_Ranger: Most nights.

FleetwdLvr05: Same. I think too much.

Mustang_Ranger: Thinking's overrated.

FleetwdLvr05: Spoken like someone who's running from it.

Mustang_Ranger: Maybe I am.

FleetwdLvr05: Maybe I am too

Mustang_Ranger: So, what are these thoughts that keep you up

FleetwdLvr05: Mostly running through things that happened during the day. Things I should have said. Things I shouldn't have done.

Mustang_Ranger: All regrets?

FleetwdLvr05: No. Just tired of always playing it safe.

Mustang_Ranger: Then stop doing that. Tomorrow, do one thing that scares you.

FleetwdLvr05: I will!

I hope she reports back and tells me what she did.

chapter
four

CRUZ

The garage smells like old coffee and hot metal. A box fan rattles in the corner, doing a whole lot of nothing against the Texas heat. Despite the fact that technically it's Fall. Texas didn't get the memo.

Wrenches hang on a pegboard in soldier-straight rows, floor striped with cords and shadow. If I had sense, I'd come at dawn, drop the van, and avoid the one person who makes me forget every good intention I've stacked like sandbags.

But I evidently don't have any sense. Bringing Flynn along isn't helping; he's already distracted, talking to Jude about a security upgrade. Tech nerd.

Juliette Winslow is half-folded into the engine compartment of a lifted F-150, one knee on the bumper, grey-grease-stained coveralls tied at her waist, revealing a clingy black tank.

She doesn't see me. Good. I should back out. Go talk to Jude myself and not stand here staring at her ass.

"Need something, Romeo?" she calls without turning. Bright voice, full of sunshine and a grin I can actually hear. She heard the guys calling me that once, and it's been her name for me ever since.

"Just a once-over on the van," I say. "I'm heading south tomorrow to pick up some refugees."

She straightens and tugs a pale blonde braid over her shoulder. Wide blue eyes meet mine, a genuine smile in place.

Fuck she's pretty.

Too young! I try to repeat that in my head like a fucking mantra.

But her lips are moving, which means she's talking.

"How many?" she asks again.

"Technically, four on the manifest. But one of them was rescued from a puppy farm and she's pregnant. They think she could deliver any day now." I swipe at the back of my neck. "So it could be more than four." I keep my words clipped and my gaze anywhere but on the smear of grease on her jaw that my fingers itch to wipe away.

"Copy that." She gives me a salute with her wrench. "I'll get you road-ready. Jude!" she yells toward the office. "Cruz is here."

So she does know my actual name. Having her call me Romeo rankles, but hearing my given name on her lips is way worse. A door creaks, and her brother steps out, wiping his hands on a rag.

"I can see that, Juliette," Jude says. He jabs his thumb in Flynn's direction. "Flynn is here too."

"You're so cranky when Emory is out of town," Juliette says. "Next time, go with her."

"And leave you and our idiot cousins in charge? I don't think so."

"Romero," Jude says. He clasps my hand and I swear he squeezes just a little too tightly. If Flynn said anything to him, I will kick his ass.

"Winslow," I say. "Just need the van looked over before I leave town in the morning."

Jude looks back at his sister. "You want me to do it?"

"I've got it," she says, already lifting the hood to take a peek.

"There's coffee," she says, her voice partially muffled. "Fair warning: it's awful. I tried a new brand because Sofia said we needed to 'elevate the experience.'"

"Cruz only drinks girly coffee," Flynn says.

Juliette peeks at him over the hood. She quirks one eyebrow.

"No offense."

"Shut the fuck up," I mutter to him.

Dane: ETA for Beaumont run tomorrow?

Me: Wheels up 0600. At the garage now getting her checked over.

Flynn: He means he's checking her out.

I shoot him a glare.

Dane: Intake room is cleared. 4 crates set. I'll be there to help you unload. Don't let Liam reorganize my labels again.

Liam: Your labels are a crime scene.

Evan: Remember to get shelter records signed. If the shepherd is the heartworm-positive one, I left meds in your go-bag. Dosage is highlighted.

Beau: Got you a full gas card in the visor, my dude. And I put a case of the good jerky under the bench seat. Not that peppered shoe leather you pretend to like.

Me: I like the peppered shoe leather. Copy on meds, records, crate count. Gas card noted.

"Bad news?" Juliette asks. Somehow, she's standing close now.

"Just the guys," I say. "They get chatty when

they know I'm leaving town."

"Bunch of mother hens," she teases.

"Something like that." Found family doesn't begin to cover it. None of us are good at goodbyes, even for twelve hours.

Jude's voice floats up from beneath the van. "Everything checks out from here."

"I told you I was taking care of it," Juliette says.

Jude slides back out, and his sister kicks his shoe. "Hey," he says, coming to his feet. "Be nice."

"I'm always nice," she says.

"You used to be nice. Now you've gotten mean like your sisters."

"They're your sisters too," she says.

Jude shudders, then looks at me. "You got sisters, Romero?"

"Nope. Only child."

"Lucky bastard."

Juliette leans in over my engine from this side of the van.

I should move. Go for a walk. A swim. Anything.

But I'm too late. Her sweet scent of oranges

and spice hit my nose, and I swallow a groan. I move quickly away. “Gotta make a phone call,” I mutter, then step out of the garage bay and back into the heat.

chapter five

JULIETTE

Sofia: I can see you staring at his ass from across the street.

Me: Whatever. Don't you have some hair to dye?

Sofia: Doing highlights, actually.

Me: He has a spectacular ass.

Sofia: All of those military boys do.

Me: True, I suppose.

Sofia: What are you going to do about it?

Me: About what?

Sofia: Your crush on Mr. Tall, Dark, and Brooding.

Me: He doesn't brood. He's just more serious than some other guys.

Me: And I don't have a crush.

Sofia: Oh, okay. Sure.

Me: I am thinking of doing something kinda crazy though.

Sofia: I'm bringing Aria in for this.

Aria: What's up?

Sofia: Juliette is thinking of doing something kinda crazy.

Aria: Wearing two different colored socks isn't crazy.

Me: Give me a little credit.

Aria: Okay, wearing no socks isn't crazy.

Me: Maybe not crazy, but it's gross. It's not like I can wear sandals to work!

Sofia: Can we focus here? What is the crazy?

Me: Romeo is going on a run tomorrow to pick up some dogs displaced by that recent storm.

Me: I think I'm going to go with him.

Aria: Did he invite you?

Me: Uh… no. He begrudgingly talks to me.

Sofia: It's because he wants you.

Me: Sure.

Me: I was thinking more along the lines of sneaking into the van and hiding there until we're too far away for him to turn around.

Sofia: And then you plan to seduce him?

Me: What? NO!

Me: I have the opportunity to meet that guy I've been chatting with on the dating app.

Me: We agreed to meet on neutral ground.

Aria: Don't you think Romeo will be pissed when he finds out you used him to go see another guy?

Sofia: Seriously. That would piss me off.

Me: No. Because he doesn't see me that way.

Me: Do I have a bit of a crush on him? Obviously. He's gorgeous and strong and steadfast and…

Me: But that's the point. It's a stupid crush that is going nowhere.

Me: Meeting this other guy in person might be just what I need to get Romeo out of my head.

Aria: Hmmmm…

Sofia: Okay, so we're looking at Road Trip as far as tropes.

Me: Y'all, for real. This is not a romance novel. I don't need a trope. I need to get out of town for just a bit and meet someone new.

Aria: I don't think this is going to go the way you want it to go.

Sofia: Same.

Me: Y'all agree on something?

Me: Hold on, I'm going to go check for signs of a Biblical plague.

Sofia: Ha-Ha.

Aria: You sound like Jude.

Me: Unlike the two of you, I don't think that's necessarily a bad thing. Jude is the best.

Me: Except when he's giving me the stink eye when he catches me ogling Romeo.

chapter six

CRUZ

I'm halfway to Houston when my phone pings with an alert. It's time for me to stop and stretch my legs anyway—before my bad knee decides to start misbehaving—so I pull off at one of the Texas supersized gas stations. The cheerful beaver sign looms like a giant sun in the sky.

Normally, these places are far too people-infested for my comfort, but they are very dog-friendly, so I've made my peace with being a customer. Besides, they have clean bathrooms and an amazing coffee bar.

I pull my phone from my pocket before going inside. I should deal with whatever this is before being assaulted by a horde of hungry Texans.

Buttercup: I did something. I need you to promise me you won't be mad.

I frown, staring at my phone, wondering if I've conjured her out of thin air.

Why would she even have my number, let alone be texting me?

Though obviously, I must have saved her contact info myself, because no one else would have saved her under that name.

A quick scan of previous texts shows a couple of conversations from months ago about the work her family's shop has done on my van. Which makes sense. Because I know her in a professional capacity. Related to automotive care.

And not in any way related to my borderline creepy obsession with her.

So then why is she texting me? And why now?

Me: Are you okay?

Me: Is something wrong?

Buttercup: Yes, I'm fine. Safe.

Me: Why would I be mad?

Buttercup: Because it affects you.

Me: I don't understand.

Buttercup: Promise you won't get mad.

Me: At you? I could never be mad at you.

Buttercup: Just promise.

Me: Okay, I promise.

Buttercup: Surprise! I'm here with you.

Me: What?

I glance around outside the van and only see a steady stream of traffic and people.

Me: Is that a secret code for something?

Buttercup: No, silly. I'm here. In the van.

Buttercup: Like a stowaway.

"Fuck." I open the door and storm across the pavement to the back of the van, where the built-in kennels are.

She's sitting against one of the crates and gives me a little wave with a smile. "Surprise."

I pinch the bridge of my nose.

"You promised you wouldn't get mad."

"Yep," I say, the p making a popping noise. "I need more context, Buttercup, because I don't know what's going on."

She kinda of crabwalks to the door, and I help her get out of the van. "I wanted to get out of town for a tiny bit. I knew if I asked, you'd probably say no."

"I would have," I grumble.

She shrugs. "See?"

"So you waited until I was too far away to turn around to reveal yourself?"

"Something like that."

I blow out a breath. "What exactly is your plan?"

"I have a friend I'm going to meet up with for dinner. Then tomorrow, I'll be another two hands to help out with the dogs."

I stare at her. Fuck, she's pretty. Her long blonde hair is pulled up in space buns--I think they're called--and she's wearing a black t-shirt with a wrench image on it. Surrounding the tool it says: *I'm here because you broke something.*

"Are you mad?" she asks.

"No, Buttercup, I'm not mad. Just fucking confused." I turn away from her. "I'm going inside to get coffee. I'll be back."

"Oh, I'm going in with you. I need to use the little girls' room, and I hear they have the best snacks." She skips up next to me to match my stride.

Skips!

As if I needed another reminder that she's way too young for me.

Twenty minutes later, we're back in the van, loaded down with snacks and matching happy beaver pajama pants. I'm still not sure how that happened, except that apparently she'd never been far enough away from Saddle Creek to have visited the famous travel-stop gas stations that litter our state.

She was so excited, I couldn't refuse. When she looked at me with those big green eyes, the idea of matching pants seemed like a great idea.

She's up in the passenger seat now that she no longer has to hide. Her feet are up on the dashboard. I've never seen her bare feet before, since she wears work boots at the garage. But there they are... cute and feminine with chipped pink polish on each nail.

She opens a bag of something, and the scent fills the cab immediately identifying her snack.

"Tell me that's not Funyuns," I say.

She grins, completely unashamed. "They're tasty, salty goodness."

I grunt, mostly because it keeps me from grinning back at her.

"They're crunchy," she argues. "Satisfying."

"They taste like sadness and dead leaves. With salt."

She laughs, the sound bubbling out like she can't help it. "Okay. If your taste buds are so much more refined, what's your road trip snack of choice?"

I hold up my gas station prize. "Beef jerky. Original flavor. The backbone of America."

She makes a face. "That's not a snack, that's punishment."

"It's protein."

"It's *leathery meat strips.*"

I grin. "You say that like it's a bad thing."

"Because it is! You could've chosen chips, candy, trail mix—but no. You went full survivalist."

"Hey, if we break down in the middle of nowhere, you'll be grateful I came prepared."

She pretends to consider that. "Fine. But if I'm dying of boredom first, I'm eating your jerky out of spite."

I glance over. "You sure you're not already doing that?"

She shoots me a look. "You're lucky I like a challenge."

I chuckle, and for a few miles, the cab fills with the sound of her crunching and me pretending not to watch the way the corners of her mouth lift every time she catches me looking.

"So what's your go-to comfort movie?" she asks, glancing at me over her sunglasses.

"*Die Hard.* Probably."

She snorts. "Of course. Explosions and masculinity. How original."

"Excuse me, *Die Hard* is a Christmas classic. Not to mention a love story."

"Because nothing says 'holiday cheer' like Bruce Willis crawling through air ducts."

"Exactly. What's yours?"

"*You've Got Mail.*"

"Figures."

"What's that supposed to mean?"

"Just—you strike me as a Meg Ryan kind of girl. Optimistic. Big feelings. Probably cry over bookstore closures."

She gasps. "Who doesn't cry over bookstore closures?"

Why the fuck couldn't she be harder to like? Or immature and silly? But a woman who reads? Who loves bookstores? That's my fucking catnip.

I sigh. "That's fair."

"Besides, she has that whole speech about how books you read when you're a child become part of your identity in a way that books you read as an adult don't. It's a perfect moment because it's so honest."

"I grew up reading The Narnia Chronicles and then Harry Potter. So I get that sentiment."

"Wait, did you say that *Die Hard* is a love story?" she asks.

"John McClane literally walks barefoot on broken glass for love."

She laughs. "That's not love, that's poor planning."

I can't help grinning at her. "You're a brat."

"Maybe." She shrugs.

We're quiet for a couple of miles.

"You know," she says, "if we combined our movie choices, we'd have something pretty good. Explosions *and* emotions."

I glance at her, and she's smiling just enough to make my chest feel tight. "Story of my life," I say. "Blowing things up and pretending it's fine."

She tilts her head, studying me for a beat too long. Then, softly: "Is that what you did in the military? Blow things up?"

"Among other things."

Up ahead, a billboard catches her attention. She points at it, excitement sparking. "World's Largest Armadillo! Next exit. Oh, we *have* to stop."

I'm already moving into the right lane. "We're really stopping to see an oversized armadillo?"

"Not oversized. *World's largest.* There's a difference."

"You realize that's code for 'sad concrete sculpture next to a gas station,' right?"

"That's the charm!" she says. "You can't do a proper road trip without at least one questionable roadside attraction."

I shake my head, but I'm already slowing down. "You're going to be so disappointed."

She leans back, smug. "You just don't understand joy."

When we pull into the gravel lot, she's practically bouncing in her seat. The "World's Largest Armadillo" is, predictably, precisely what I said —cracked cement, faded paint, one beady eye missing.

She still gasps like it's the Eiffel Tower.

"Oh, he's perfect," she whispers reverently. "Look at that craftsmanship."

"Pretty sure that craftsmanship involved some guy with two first names and a mullet," I mutter.

She swats my arm, but still giggles. "Don't ruin it. Go stand next to him so I can take a picture."

"I'm not posing with a mutant armadillo."

"Come on," she pleads, her smile turning just a little too sweet. "For the memories."

And just like that, I'm standing next to this cracked concrete creature while she lines up her phone, trying not to look like an idiot.

She snaps the photo, then checks it, and rolls her eyes. "You could smile."

I grab her and pull her to stand with me in front of the mutant armadillo. Then I hold up her phone and take a selfie of us.

She looks at that photo and releases a sigh. "That's much better. Thank you."

I choose not to analyze why my smile looks so goddamn real in the picture with her.

chapter seven

JULIETTE

Cruz Romero, AKA Romeo, is hot as hell.

He's got a ball cap on backwards today, his thick dark hair curls around the edges of the hat. The black whiskey t-shirt he's wearing looks so soft, I'm dying to touch it. And it should be considered indecent the way it's molded to Cruz's broad, muscular torso. His worn jeans are slung low on his hips and perfectly highlight his ass.

I've been so wrapped up in looking at him and talking to him that I haven't even checked on a response from Ranger. I hope he can meet tonight. I sent him a message earlier today from the back of the van before I outed myself to my unsuspecting chauffeur.

Meeting Ranger will hopefully cool my slight obsession with my travel companion.

Cruz clears his throat. “Alright, we’ve communed with the sacred armadillo. Back on the road?”

I nod. “Sounds good. We still have a couple of hours, right?”

“Yeah. If traffic cooperates,” he says.

I want to know everything about this man, but I obviously can’t ask him a million questions. Road trip games to the rescue. “New game,” I say.

“Oh no,” he groans dramatically. “Last time you said that, I ended up posing with a one-eyed armadillo.”

“This one doesn’t involve potential tetanus. Promise.”

He grins at me and I swear my heart does a double beat.

“Alright, Buttercup, what’s the game?”

“It’s simple. This or that. No explanations. Just instinct.”

He chuckles. “And if I refuse?”

I sniff. "You'll hurt my delicate feelings."

"Ah, emotional blackmail. Got it. Fine, hit me."

I clap my hands, happy he's going to indulge me. "Okay. Coffee or tea?"

"Coffee."

"Morning or night?"

"Night."

"Beach or mountains?"

"Mountains. But why aren't you answering the same questions?"

"Oh, right. Coffee, morning, and beach. Dogs or cats?"

"Dogs."

I snort. "Duh. I like both. No preference, just something furry in my lap, please and thank you."

"I don't hate cats," he says.

"Okay, Star Wars or Star Trek?"

He scoffs as if the question itself is offensive. "Star Wars. No contest."

"Really? I would've pegged you as a Trekkie."

"Because I seem like the kind of guy who enjoys complicated ethical debates in space?"

"Exactly."

"I mean, I do. But lightsabers, come on. Not

to mention Chewbacca. Really, unfair comparison."

"Agreed. Next one—cake or pie?"

"Pie. Every time."

"Incorrect," I say. "Cake wins because frosting exists."

"Yeah, but pie has crust. You can't trust people who don't like crust."

I stare at his profile for a minute. "Crust versus frosting? Sir, that does not even make sense."

"I mean, I'm not saying I don't like frosting. I just really like pie."

I giggle. "Bygones. Okay, moving on. Vampires or zombies?"

"Zombies."

"Same," I say.

"Really? No sparkling vampires for you?"

"Uh, no. I never could get into those books. That heroine was like a piece of unbuttered toast. Just sad and boring."

"Plus zombie movies," he says.

"Definitely. *Warm Bodies*, *World War Z*, *Zombieland*, both the first and the sequel," I say.

"More opportunities for humor. Vampires take themselves far too seriously," he says.

"Yes! That's totally what it is."

"See, I know things," he says.

"No doubt you know a lot of things. Even if it doesn't involve explosions or dogs."

"I make a mean pot of chili, too."

"Good to know. Speaking of food, are you a jerky snack guy in general or just on road trips?"

"I appreciate jerky any time. But mostly this particular one." He holds up his bag. "Don't tell Beau. He likes this gourmet jerky and packed some in the van for me. But I prefer—"

"The shoe leather," I answer for him.

"Yes. I want to work for my flavor."

I laugh.

"You? Salty or sweet on a road trip?" he asks.

"Salty in the car, sweet everywhere else." I clear my throat. "Okay, last one. Be honest."

"Always."

"Would you rather know what people are thinking or be invisible?"

"Invisible," he says, no hesitation.

"So you could sneak around?" I ask, unable to hide my curiosity.

"Nah, I just sometimes need a break from people," he admits. "What about you?"

"I think I'd like to know what people are

thinking. But only if I could turn it off. I think that power could get overwhelming very quickly."

"Possibly. But some people don't have two thoughts to rub together."

I chuckle. "Well, that's true."

I am in trouble, I know that much. I force myself to pick up my phone and check in the app.

Mustang_Ranger: Sounds great. I'll see you then.

Mustang_Ranger: Looking forward to finally meeting you.

FleetwdLvr05: Me too!

And I am. That's not a lie. I just know that tonight will more than likely be a disappointment. I'm sure Ranger is a great guy. But I know he's not Cruz and that thought just makes me already feel like the date is a failure.

chapter
eight

CRUZ

The last hour of the car ride was tense.

For me. I don't think Buttercup noticed.

It started after we finished playing her last game. She put a playlist on. It was all stuff I like, stuff I listen to. Which, I knew, obviously from the first time I saw her at the garage singing *Drift Away*.

But this particular playlist was more specific than that. It was at least eighty percent Fleetwood Mac.

They were a very successful, very popular

band. But she knew every word to every one of their songs.

Just like *FleetwdLvr05*.

Coincidence? Maybe.

But there was more. She's meeting a friend tonight.

That could be a coincidence, sure.

On more than one occasion, she typed something on her phone, and my phone—hidden in my jeans pocket—would vibrate with an alert.

All of it could mean nothing. Or maybe it means everything.

We've checked into the hotel for the night. One room. One bed. Because, of course, that's how this would all go. It makes sense. All the hotels in the area are packed with people who've been displaced by the recent storm. We're lucky that Liam called ahead and reserved a room for me when we knew I'd have to make this trip.

I don't know whether to hope I'm wrong or be grateful I'm right.

She is currently in the bathroom getting ready. Ready to meet her friend.

It's time to bring in reinforcements. I don't want to air all of this to the entire team, so I create a new text between me, Liam, and Flynn.

. . .

Me: SOS!

Liam: What's up, brother?

Me: First... Juliette is with me.

Me: In Houston.

Liam: Jude is gonna kick your ass.

Me: Probably. But she hid in the van and didn't tell me she was with me until more than halfway into the drive.

Flynn: I'm here. What did I miss?

Flynn: Oh damn!

Me: Yeah. I haven't gotten to the problem portion of my SOS.

Flynn: I can't tell if I'm nervous or excited on your behalf.

Me: You know that chick I've been chatting with on the dating app?

Liam: You've mentioned her a couple of times.

Me: I think she might be Juliette.

Flynn: Wait, what?

Liam: He thinks his online girlfriend IS Juliette.

Flynn: No shit? Really?

Me: There are just a lot of coincidences.

Liam: This is good news, though. Right?

Liam: Both of the women you're interested in are the same person.

Flynn: Does seem pretty damn perfect.

Me: But is it?

Liam: Tell me this… what is it about the woman online that caught your attention?

Me: She's very easy to talk to.

Me: Obviously intelligent because she's witty.

Me: I feel a connection that I can't even explain.

Me: Which sounds stupid, I know.

Flynn: Not stupid at all.

Flynn: That's how it always felt with Temple.

Liam: Wren too.

Me: Yeah, but y'all already knew those women.

Me: I barely know Juliette.

Me: And let's not forget that she's too young for me.

Liam: You're both adults.

Flynn: Yep. Seems like if they are the same woman, you've got your answer right there.

Then she comes out of the bathroom looking so damn sexy. Her hair is down, falling around her shoulders in a blonde waterfall of glossy waves. She's got make-up on. Nothing particularly bold, but her eyes look more intense, her irises bluer, her lashes darker.

Rather than coveralls or blue jeans, she's

wearing a dress. One that accents every one of her thick curves. I swallow hard. I know I'm staring, cataloging every part of her, but I can't help it. Can't look away.

"You look gorgeous," I blurt.

She smiles. "Thank you, Cruz. That means a lot. Truly."

Her eyes lock and a moment passes between us where everything feels heavy and... expectant? As if she's wanting me to say something else, but I don't know what it is.

"I'll walk you down," I tell her.

"You don't have to," she says.

"A man's gotta eat."

"True."

"So what time is your friend supposed to meet you?" I ask.

She folds her lips in. "I have a confession."

"What's that?"

"Do you think you can call someone you've never met in person a friend?"

"Yeah, I don't see why not. That's how lots of people used to meet. Pen pals and letters and whatever. Now, things are just more immediate."

She smiles. "Yes, like a pen pal."

"That who you're meeting?" I ask. Though

this conversation feels wrong, like I'm lying to her. But I still don't know for sure that she's my Fleetwood.

"I guess you could say that. We met on a dating app. Is that weird?"

"Plenty of people meet that way now. It might have been weird many years ago, but it's a viable way to meet people these days."

"Oh. I guess that's true." She bites down on her lip. "Have you ever done it? Online dating?"

I nod. "Once or twice."

We walk to the elevator and then ride down to the lobby. The restaurant and bar combo isn't big, but it beats going out after you've been on the road all day. It occurs to me that aside from the quick shower I took when we arrived, I didn't get ready like I'm going on a date.

She will probably be disappointed that it's me. Once she knows, she can move on to someone else. No doubt, she's been chatting with other guys on there. Men closer to her age with two perfectly functioning knees that don't ache when the wind changes directions.

I leave her with the hostess, telling her to text me if she needs something, then I walk away.

I need a moment to think through what I'm

about to do. I'm not exactly worried about ruining our friendship. Aside from this trip, we've not been alone together except, on occasion, in the garage. But I do know I don't want to fuck this up.

In all my years, I've never felt like this about another woman. Juliette hits all of my targets, rings all of my bells, or whatever the fuck a proper metaphor is. I just know that she's not only physically attractive, she's smart, funny, talented, and kind—the whole damn package.

I make my way to the concierge desk and ask if there is any way I can get some emergency flowers. The woman laughs, but makes a call.

"You're in luck," she says. "We had a wedding that was supposed to happen here last night, but the groom's parents lost their house in the storm, so they've postponed the ceremony."

"Well, that doesn't sound very lucky," I say.

"No. They've had terrible luck, poor kids. But the flowers for the wedding were already delivered and are sitting in a fridge. I don't think they'll miss one of the table centerpieces. They're just long-stem red roses."

About this time, a guy comes around the

corner carrying a couple of vases. "I didn't know if you wanted options," he tells the concierge.

"Perfect. Thanks," she tells the guy. Then she looks at me. "Pick your poison, darlin."

I take the roses out of both vases and retie the bow so they make one bouquet. "This will work perfectly." I pull a couple of bills out of my wallet and pass them to her. "Thank you."

She smiles. "Good luck."

"Yeah, I might need it." Then I make my way back to the restaurant. Juliette is still sitting at the table, but her smile isn't as bright. She probably thinks she's being stood up.

My legs eat up the distance to her table and then I slide into the booth across from her.

Her eyes widen, then she frowns.

"FleetwdLvr05?" I ask.

Her lips part.

I set the roses down on the table and hold my hand out to her. "I'm Mustang_Ranger."

chapter nine

JULIETTE

The low murmur of the restaurant feels distant, like I'm underwater. Forks clink against plates, laughter drifts from the bar, and yet all I can hear is the pounding of my pulse in my ears.

I stare at him, his words not quite registering in my brain. "I don't understand," I manage, shaking my head. "Is this some kind of a joke?"

He leans back against his side of the booth, the soft light catching the gold in his eyes. "No," he says quietly. "Not a joke. I only just figured it out myself."

The air between us tightens. I can't seem to

stop staring—his dark beard, the sharp angles of his jaw, the faint sprinkle of gray at his temples. His eyes—golden brown, thoughtful, infuriatingly calm—pin me in place. The collar of his T-shirt dips low enough to reveal a triangle of chest hair, and I hate that I notice it right now of all times.

He clears his throat. "You are FleetwdLvr05, right?"

The name hits me like a spark to dry tinder.

I nod slowly. "The app just matched us? And we've been talking this whole time... not knowing we already knew each other?"

"Yep." The word lands with a heavy pop of his lips.

My face burns. "How did you figure it out?"

"Mostly your playlist in the car," he says.

"Damn Stevie Nicks," I mumble. "Her music really does connect souls, huh?"

He gives a small, crooked smile. "Are you disappointed?"

I blink at him. "No. Not at all. I mean—come on, you have to have noticed how much of a crush I have on you. I haven't exactly been covert."

"Maybe not," he admits, his voice low,

rough. "But your brother has made it very clear that you're off-limits."

That earns a bitter laugh from me. "That might've worked in his favor a couple of years ago. But I've been an adult for a while now. He just doesn't want to admit it."

Something flickers in his expression—something that looks dangerously like want, desire... need. Then it's gone.

"Why don't you ever call me by my first name?" I ask the question before I can stop it.

His jaw tightens. "Because then I have to admit there's something here. Something between us."

"Because every Romeo needs his Juliette?"

He huffs a breath, shaking his head. "Something like that."

I lean in, my voice soft but sharp. "I would not have taken you for a coward."

His eyes lift to mine, slow and deliberate. "This isn't about fear."

I cock a brow. "Isn't it, though?"

"No," he says, too calm. "It's about right and wrong."

His words stab at my tender heart. "You think it's wrong to want to be with me?"

"I'm old enough to be your father."

I roll my eyes. "You are not my father."

"I'm very well aware of that. But our age difference is significant."

"Is that all you've got? Clinging to the age argument?"

"It matters," he insists.

"To whom? Not me. The only person it matters to is you."

He drags a hand through his hair, exhaling hard. "What about Jude?"

"What about him?" I shoot back. "In case you haven't noticed, I'm a grown woman."

"Trust me," he says, voice dipping an octave, "that hasn't escaped my attention." His eyes flick for just a second to my cleavage.

The way he says it sends a pulse of heat through my chest. My fingers twitch on the table. "Then give me one actual reason. One real reason you don't want to be with me."

"Juliette—"

"No, I'm serious. You don't like my personality? You hate that I usually have grease under my fingernails? You think my ass is too big? My hair too long? My taste in music too basic?"

"Fuck, Buttercup—" His voice cracks.

"There's nothing wrong with you. This is all about me."

The nickname slams into me, both familiar and forbidden.

"So you get to just make the decision for both of us?" I hiss. I stand, and he follows me.

The air crackles. People at nearby tables glance over. The server hesitates by the bar. My face burns.

"Come on," he mutters. "Let's not do this here."

Before I can say anything else, he drops bills on the table, grabs the roses and my wrist, and pulls me out of the restaurant. He says something to the waitress on the way out.

My heart is slamming itself against my chest. Pound, pound, pound. I wait until we're enclosed in the elevator.

"I don't get a say in what I want?" I jab a finger into his chest, feeling the solid warmth beneath the thin fabric of his shirt. "Don't you dare tell me I'm too young to know what I want."

He towers over me. His hand is still tight around my wrist. "I'll probably die before you even have gray hair."

I scoff. "Good! I'll still be hot for my second husband."

His jaw flexes. "Second husband? I don't fucking think so."

"You don't want me, you don't get a say in who gets me," I shoot back, voice trembling—not with fear, but fury.

"I never said I didn't want you," he growls. "Only that I *shouldn't* want you."

The hallway smells faintly of old wood and lemon cleaner. The carpet muffles our steps, but not the silence stretching between us.

Inside our room, the door clicks shut behind us. The low lamplight paints him in amber and shadows. He turns, rakes a hand through his hair again, and exhales hard.

"This," he says, "is exactly why I didn't want to start something."

I cross my arms. "Then why did you?"

He opens his mouth, then closes it. His eyes move over me—frustration, hunger, regret, all tangled up.

"Say it," I whisper.

He swallows. "Because you make me forget how to be careful."

My heart stutters. "Then stop pretending you don't want me."

He takes one step forward. Then another. When he's close enough that I can smell the faint salt of his skin and the citrus of his soap, I look up at him and say quietly, "You called me Buttercup."

His lips twitch. "Old habits."

"Bad ones," I murmur.

He nods slowly. "The worst."

And still, neither of us moves away.

"Why Buttercup?"

"You reminded me of Princess Buttercup the first time I saw you." He fingers a strand of my blonde hair. He shrugs. "When I found out your name, I just couldn't make myself use it."

"As far as nicknames go, Buttercup is a nice one. Shall I call you Farm Boy?"

He chuffs a laugh. "As you wish."

The space between us is all pulse and static.

He's close enough that the air feels warmer, the hotel air conditioning humming uselessly behind him.

"We shouldn't do this," he says, but he doesn't move.

"Do what, exactly?" I wait.

His eyes search my face, land on my lips. He gives a quiet, helpless laugh. "You have no idea how much I want you."

"You could show me."

He looks at me then—really looks—and something in his eyes softens. "Juliette..." My name sounds like it hurts coming out of his mouth.

His fingers twitch at his sides before he lets them hover, just barely, at my waist. Not touching. Just there. The heat from his skin ghosts across the fabric of my dress, and every nerve I have lights up.

"Say it again," I whisper.

He shakes his head once. "That's the problem. Every time I say your name, it feels like a promise I can't keep."

I swallow hard. "Maybe stop thinking about what could go wrong and think about what could go right."

He gives a low, disbelieving laugh, the sound rough as gravel. "Don't mistake my reluctance for ignorance. I have zero doubts about how good things would be between us."

Another ghost of a touch, this time the

denim of his jeans as he closes the distance between our bodies.

For one impossible second, everything narrows to that—his breath against my cheek, the scent of his soap and the hotel shampoo, the heat between us. I could lean forward half an inch and end this standoff forever.

Then there's a knock on the door. Sharp. Intrusive.

We both flinch.

He steps back first, runs a hand through his hair. The distance hits like cold air. "Room service," a voice calls from the hall.

He doesn't answer. I can't seem to breathe.

Finally, he mutters, "I asked them to bring our orders up here."

"I guess you've been saved by the bell or something," I say, my voice sounding sharper than intended.

chapter **ten**

CRUZ

I let the room service guy in, and he rolls the cart over by the desk. Juliette is still standing where I left her. I sign the check, giving the guy a nice tip before locking the door behind him. I take a deep breath before turning back around.

She's got her arms wrapped around herself as if she needs a hug, and that's the only one available. Recognizing that makes my entire body ache with the need to fix everything in her life.

"What about other guys from the app?" I ask.

She frowns. "What other guys?" She tosses

her arms up. "There are no other guys. You know, for being so old and mature, you're a dumbass. There is only you. I mean, there was *you* and *computer you,* which I obviously didn't know was the same person. But the only reason I even got on that stupid app was because you made it abundantly clear that you were not for me."

"You just have a lot of life you haven't lived. You might think you want me, but you could change your mind. Realize you want to explore the world, date around."

I shake my head the entire time he's talking because he clearly hasn't been paying attention.

"Juliette—" I start, but she interrupts me.

"No." She holds a hand up. "Now is my turn to talk. I don't remember a lot about my parents, but I remember sitting in my mother's lap and talking to her. She was so patient with any and all of my questions. She would smile and every time she would tell me, 'Y ou have a beautiful old soul, my sweet Juliette, just like your father. Don't let anyone steal that from you.'"

Juliette kicks off her shoes and paces the space between the bed and the window. "It took me a long time to realize what she meant. Since then, other people have said similar things to me. My sisters tease me for being a stodgy old lady. I guess some people would call it wisdom, but I think what people see in me, why people say that, is because there is a—"

"A stillness about you," I say. "You're settled, comfortable in your skin the way some people never are. You have a quiet strength that I noticed immediately. Admittedly, after I noticed your hair and your ass."

She smirks at me.

I close the distance between us. "You think I don't see all of that in you?" I squeeze her biceps. "Of course, I see you. How could I not?"

"Then why do you question whether what I feel for you is real or lasting?" she asks. "If you truly saw me, you'd know."

"What would I know?"

"That I'm the Juliette to your Romeo. Only the Taylor Swift version, not the Shakespearean tragedy. I'm not a fanciful teenage girl. I see all of you, Cruz Romero. From your tender heart taking care of all of those dogs with your buddies to the way you wince and try to hide your limp when it rains."

"Oh, for fuck's sake," I say, rubbing at the back of my neck.

"I don't need to travel the world or date other men to know that you are the one I want."

I shake my head. "You going to be stubborn about this?"

"I will fight for you, but only if you'd do the same for me. If you're not willing to risk everything to be with me, then you don't deserve me."

That makes me smile. "I love how fierce you are. How brave and unapologetic."

"Then stop pushing me away. Stop making excuses. If you want me, take me."

I don't wait any longer. I lower my mouth and take her lips. She whimpers, and I growl as our tongues meet. Then she's kissing me, making greedy little noises at the back of her throat. My cock is a steel bar in my jeans.

I grip her bottom, pressing her body against the wall. Now my hard cock is up against her center. She hooks a leg around my hip, opening herself to me. Her dress makes this all the more convenient. I rock my erection against her, feeling the heat of her fabric-covered pussy through the denim of my jeans.

She gasps and pulls back. "You're hard?"

"I'm always hard around you."

Her smile is wide and bright. "I knew you wanted me."

"Fuck yeah, I want you."

"Show me," she says. There's a challenge heating her eyes, and damned if it doesn't turn me on even more.

I pull off my t-shirt, dropping it somewhere on the hotel floor behind me. I start on my jeans, unbuttoning and then unzipping them to give my dick some breathing room.

She's got her dress undone and slides it off her body. Black lace-covered breasts and matching panties.

"Fuck, Buttercup. Look at you."

"I want you to look at me, Cruz. I want you to like what you see."

"I love what I see. You're so goddamn beautiful."

She reaches behind her back and unhooks her bra, then it falls to the floor between us. Her perfect tits are heavy and hard-tipped, and begging for attention.

"Panties off," I instruct. I kick off my jeans, but leave my boxers in place for the time being.

She peels off those lace panties, then stands

before me, completely bared. I've never seen anything more beautiful in my life.

"Put one foot up here." I lift her leg so she can brace her foot on the edge of the desk. "Open yourself to me. Let me see all that slick."

She gasps, but follows my instructions.

My mouth waters at the sight of her pink pussy and the pale blonde hair she keeps trimmed above her mound.

"I'm going to fucking lose my mind if I don't get my mouth on you soon," I say. I fall to my knees in front of her. "Look what you've been hiding in those coveralls. Walking around that garage with this fucking perfect pussy right between your legs."

"Cruz," she whimpers.

I say nothing, leaning forward to suck her clit into my mouth. I'm too impatient for finesse or seduction. I want her come on my tongue right the fuck now.

Her nails rake across my scalp as she digs into my hair.

I plunge one and then a second finger into her hot, slick channel, and she nearly collapses against the wall.

"Oh my God," she whispers.

I fuck her with those fingers and pull my mouth back to watch her. Her toes curl, and her eyes squeeze shut.

"Let go, Juliette. Come all over my face, my beard," I beg. "Let me taste your sweetness."

She whimpers again.

I slide my tongue up her pussy walls and circle her clit before pulling it into my mouth. I suck hard.

"Cruz, Cruz," she chants my name like a prayer.

I curl my fingers inside her to brush her front wall. Her legs shake as she chants my name and rocks her pussy against my face.

Then she shatters.

Her release splashes into my mouth, and I lap her up. I'm a glutton for the taste of my girl. I place small kisses around the apex of her thighs, loving the silky softness of her skin.

I stand, kissing my way up her bare body. I spend some time on her needy little nipples. "I need to know something," I say.

"What's that?"

"Are you a virgin? Do I need to be gentle with you? I'm not feeling very gentle at the moment, Juliette. You've got me so goddamn worked up I feel like a damned animal."

"Don't be gentle," she says. She moves and flings herself across the bed. "Make me yours, please."

"Answer my fucking question."

"I'm not very experienced, but no, I'm not a virgin. I did it once with a guy right after high school graduation." She leans up on her elbows. "And I have toys." She licks her lips, her eyes glued to the front of my boxers. "I think I can take you."

I raise an eyebrow. "Oh, you think you can?" I drop my boxers and grip my dick. "Think you can take me?"

"You are much bigger than anything I've used, but I've also never been this wet. Cruz, please."

"I can't wait any longer. I need to be inside you," I growl. "And I don't have any goddamn condoms because I wasn't planning on fucking anyone this weekend. So if you don't want me inside you, if you don't want me to fuck you bare, tell me now. Or I'm going to sink so deep inside you, you'll forget what life was like before me fucking you."

"I want all of that," she says. "Fuck me bare."

She spreads her legs. Then reaches up and cups both of her tits. Her back arches. "I'm aching for you."

"I've got everything you need. I'm the Romeo to your Juliette, right?"

"Yes!"

With that, I thrust into her in one swift motion. She's impossibly tight, and she cries out when I'm in her all the way to the hilt. "Did I hurt you?"

"No. I'm just really full."

"You feel like home," I say, unable to keep my mouth shut. Sinking inside her is a feeling unlike any other. She fits me like a proverbial glove.

"Fucking made for me," I growl.

She wraps her legs around my waist. "Cruz, I want to come on your dick. Can you make me come?" Her hands rub down my bare back.

I rear back, then press forward, starting a rhythm as I fuck her hard. "Yeah, I'm going to make you come all over this dick."

I shift our positions so I'm up on my knees with her plump ass resting on my thighs while I pound into her.

"You take my dick so well. Look at that." I

rub my thumb through her slick folds until I find her clit and circle it slowly.

“Ohmygod!” she yells. “Like that. So good. Don’t stop.”

I grip her hips with one hand and play with her clit with the other. My balls tighten, and pleasure shoots up my spine. I’m getting close. I already made her come once, but I want to feel her pussy milking me.

“Together,” I say. “I want you to come with me.”

She nods. “I’m so close.”

“Good, because I can’t fucking hold off anymore. You feel too damn good.” I squeeze her clit. “Now. Come now.”

And she does. In unison with me, like this is how it was supposed to be all along.

chapter **eleven**

JULIETTE

The morning light spills through the thin hotel curtains in bands of gold and white, catching dust motes that hang in the air like tiny stars. The room smells faintly of coffee, but mostly of sex. The sheets are still warm where Cruz had been next to me. Everything about the bed is in disarray.

We made love so many times last night, and my body is deliciously sore because of it.

Cruz is by the window now, leaning one shoulder against the wall, phone in his hand. He's quiet—has been since sunrise. The kind of quiet that feels full of thoughts he's not ready to say out loud.

Outside, the world is already awake. A delivery truck rattles over the uneven pavement, and someone laughs on the sidewalk below. Life goes on, even when yours has just changed shape overnight.

I sit up, wrapping the sheet around me, not because I need to, but because it feels like armor. "You're thinking too loud," I say.

He glances over, a faint smile pulling at the corner of his mouth. "Didn't realize thinking was a noise."

"With you, it's always a noise."

He sets his phone down and comes to sit at the edge of the bed, elbows on his knees. "Your brother's gonna lose his mind."

"Probably," I admit. "But he'll get over it. He always does."

He exhales, long and slow. "I don't want this to make your life harder, Juliette."

"It won't." I reach for his hand, threading my fingers through his. "It'll make it *ours.* There's a difference."

He studies our joined hands for a long

moment, thumb brushing absently over my knuckles. "You're really sure about this?"

"About you? Yeah."

He lifts his gaze, meets mine. "Then I guess that's enough. I'll slay any dragons that get in our way. Making you happy is the only thing that matters." He leans forward and kisses my forehead. "As much as I'd like to crawl into that bed with you, we've got to go pick up the dogs."

"Oh, right." I chuckle. "That was kind of your point to this whole trip, even though I hijacked it."

"It was the best hostile takeover ever."

We pack quickly after that, since there's not really much to gather. When we meet by the door, he reaches past me to hold it open, his arm brushing mine. The touch is simple, familiar, grounding.

"Ready?" he asks.

"As I'll ever be."

After picking up the dogs and ensuring they were settled in the back of the van, we did our best to make the return trip as fast as possible. Cruz dropped me off so I could get my car, and then he headed straight out to the sanctuary. Our relationship would resume later, after he got the dogs settled in their new place.

My phone pings in my pocket.

Aria: Jude knows about you and Cruz.

Well, shit. That didn't take long.

Me: How'd he find out?

Sofia: He has some legit detective skills, as it turns out.

Aria: A combination of tracking your phone and remembering that's where your man was headed.

Sofia: He's already left the garage to head to the sanctuary.

Me: Shit! Why didn't you lead with that? I gotta go.

. . .

By the time I get to the lot behind the dog sanctuary, I can hear my brother's voice before I even see him. It's the kind of low, sharp tone that makes the hair on my arms stand up—the same one he used to use when someone messed with me in high school.

"Jude!" I call, but he doesn't turn.

He's already crossing the gravel, jaw tight, shoulders squared, heading straight for Cruz, who's standing near his van. Thankfully it looks like the other guys have unloaded the dogs, and Evan and Marley are dealing with their immediate needs.

My brother advances on Cruz.

Jude has always looked like he might be mean with tattoos and piercings, but the truth is, he's always been a complete softie. Especially when it came to his sisters. And now his wife, Emory. But right now, his face is locked in an expression that gives me pause.

"Jude, stop!" I shout again, but he doesn't.

Cruz doesn't move, doesn't even blink. He just stands there, calm in that maddening way he has, watching Jude close the distance between them.

"You think this is funny?" Jude snaps. "You think it's cute, going after my kid sister like that?"

Cruz's voice is low. "I don't think any of this is funny."

"She's half your age!" Jude's face is red now, sweat glinting on his temple. "You bring your van into my shop, I fix your brakes, help you outfit it for your specific needs, and all the while you're thinking about—" He cuts himself off, glancing at me like the words are poison. "What? How to seduce my baby sister? What the hell's wrong with you?"

Cruz doesn't flinch. "Nothing's wrong with me."

"Bullshit."

The punch comes fast. A sharp crack echoes across the gravel. Cruz's head jerks to the side, but he doesn't hit back. He just wipes at his mouth with the back of his hand, checks for blood, and looks at Jude again.

"You done?" he asks quietly.

Jude shoves him, hard. "Not even close."

This is when my reinforcements arrive. Both

of my sisters and my sister-in-law. If anyone can make Jude see reason, it's Emory.

But my brother hasn't noticed their arrival. "Jude!" I rush forward, grabbing at his arm. "Stop! You're not helping anything!"

He turns on me, eyes wild. "Stay out of it, Juliette!" He reaches to pull me behind him, the way he always has, the way big brothers do. "I'll deal with you later."

Except I'm not little anymore. I yank my arm back. "Don't you dare treat me like I'm twelve!"

Cruz moves then—just one step forward, but the air shifts around him. His voice is steady, deep, and dangerous in that quiet way that makes everything stop.

"You can put your hands on me all you want," he says, low and even. "Blacken both of my eyes, bust my lip some more, break some ribs if you have to. But understand that you may not touch her like that. Or raise your voice to her. Do either of those things, and you and I are going to have serious problems."

The world goes still. The only sound is the wind rattling through the oak trees and the distant barks of the dogs from the kennels.

Jude freezes, hand half-raised, his chest heaving. The weight of Cruz's words hangs heavy in the air—no threat, just truth.

For a long second, they stare at each other. Then something in Jude's expression falters. That's when Emory approaches, puts herself between Jude and Cruz.

"Jude, baby, stop and think. Look at him."

And he does, my brother looks at Cruz—really looks—and for the first time, he sees what I've known all along.

Cruz isn't playing with me. He isn't chasing something he can't have. He's standing here, taking punches he doesn't deserve, because walking away would hurt me more.

Jude drops his hand. His voice comes out rough, low. "You really love her, don't you?"

Cruz doesn't hesitate. "Yeah. I do."

My throat tightens.

Jude exhales, shoulders sagging as the fight drains out of him. He rubs at his jaw, shaking his head. "Christ, this town's gonna have a hay day with that."

"Let them," I say.

He huffs a humorless laugh. "You just had to pick someone twice your age."

I shake my head. "I picked the right one for me. The one who sees me and loves me for who I am. That's all I ever wanted," I reply.

Jude glances between us, and for a flicker of a moment, I see something almost like acceptance. Not approval. Not yet. But maybe the first hint of it.

He mutters, "Don't make me regret not kicking your ass twice," and stalks off toward his truck, gravel crunching under his boots. Emory is at his side, speaking low to him. She glances back at me, and I give her a wave and a smile.

I hear my sisters mumbling about missing all the good drama as they climb back in their car.

When the sound fades, Cruz lets out a slow breath and looks at me. The bruise is already blooming along his jaw, deep and angry.

"You okay?" I whisper.

He stretches his jaw. "I will be. Just need some ice."

"You didn't have to let him."

"Yeah," he says, lips curving just barely. "I did."

I step closer, pressing my palm lightly against his chest, feeling his heart beat steadily beneath my hand. The tension that's been stretching between us for weeks finally settles, quiet and certain.

"I love you too, you know."

chapter **twelve**

JULIETTE

Cruz's place smells like cedar and clean laundry. It's small. One of those tiny rental cabins near the river. It fits him, though.

He's sitting at the edge of his couch when I come in, a melting ice pack pressed against the side of his jaw. The bruise has already started to darken, a wash of purple along his cheekbone.

"Looks bad," I say, setting my bag down on the chair.

He doesn't look up right away. "Feels worse."

I cross the room and kneel in front of him, reaching for the ice pack. "Let me."

He hesitates for a heartbeat, then lets me take it. The cold stings my fingers. I press it gently to his skin, watching the way his jaw flexes under the pressure.

"You didn't have to just stand there and take it," I whisper.

"I know." His voice is quiet, low enough that it almost gets lost under the hum of the air conditioner. "But it was easier than hitting your brother."

"He didn't deserve that kind of grace."

Cruz gives a tired half-smile. "Maybe not. But you love him. And you would've looked at me differently if I'd hit him back."

He's right, and I hate that he's right.

I pull the ice away for a second, tracing the edge of the bruise with my thumb. The skin is warm, rough under my touch. "Still doesn't make it okay."

"Never said it did." His gaze finds mine, steady and soft all at once. "But I'm not sorry I did it."

"Because you're noble?"

He laughs under his breath. "Hardly. Because you were there. And I'll always take the hit if it means you don't have to."

Something catches in my chest, a sharp little ache that feels a lot like love.

"You shouldn't have to protect me," I say.

He tilts his head, eyes holding mine. "If you're going to be mine, Juliette, you need to get used to it. I will always protect you. Always."

For a moment, neither of us says anything. The ice pack drips a little, cold water running over my knuckles. He reaches out, brushes his thumb across the wet trail, slow and deliberate.

"You know he's not wrong," Cruz says softly. "People are gonna talk."

"Let them," I answer, echoing what I said earlier. "This is Saddle Creek—they'll talk about anyone who buys the wrong brand of dog food. They'll get bored eventually."

He huffs out a laugh, and I feel it vibrate through him.

When I lean back to look at him, the bruise is angry but less swollen. His eyes are tired, but there's something gentler there too—something that wasn't before.

"Come here," he murmurs, tugging me forward until I'm sideways across his lap, my head tucked against his chest.

"You know it's gonna go both ways. I'm always going to protect you, too."

He chuffs a little laugh. "I have no doubt. You know, Princess Buttercup isn't as fitting as I initially thought. Maybe I should've called you Valkyrie."

"As long as you call me yours, I don't care about the rest."

The room is quiet except for the cicadas outside, the hum of the fridge, and the soft rhythm of our breathing syncing in the dark.

Right now, it's just Cruz, warm and steady, the faint smell of cedar and coffee, and the quiet, stubborn kind of peace that only comes when you stop running from what you already knew was yours.

epilogue

CRUZ

a few months later...

I'm pretty sure that the women at *Sugar Bakers* think I'm a complete lunatic. But I'm okay with that.

I told Juliette I'd be a little late coming home tonight, so hopefully she's there waiting. We don't officially live together, but she is at my little cabin more often than not.

We found a house we both love, and I heard

from the realtor today that they accepted my bid. So I get to tell her the good news.

When I pull my mustang up in front of my cabin, I smile when I catch sight of her car. She's probably inside, crashed out on the couch.

I grab my box from the bakery and head to my front door. But before I can open it, she comes rushing out with a pot in hand. Smoke billows from the pot and something that I don't recognize is melted to the sides and bottom of the cookware.

"Dammit, you're home," she says.

"Just how every man likes to be greeted by the love of his life," I say.

"I tried to make dinner."

I nod. "Is it too soon for me to ask what it was supposed to be?"

"As a matter of fact, yes, it is. Also, the cabin is smoky. I opened the windows as best I could."

"Hey, don't worry about it."

"I wanted to cook for you," she says, her lips in a little pout.

"I don't need you to cook for me. I'm Mexican, baby, I'm a great cook."

She sniffs. "You are."

"And you have other skills." I waggle my eyebrows at her.

She rolls her eyes. "I don't think blow jobs," she whispers that last part, "is relevant."

"Pretty damn relevant to me."

"What's in the pink box?"

"Ah, you finally noticed." I lead her over to the single chair I have on the tiny cabin porch. "Sit down, Valkyrie."

She sits and I put the box on her lap.

"People might think that we don't match, that we don't go together, but I don't care about any of that." I open the box. "Because we go together like frosting in a pie crust."

She looks down at the baked monstrosity in her lap, then starts laughing. "You are a lunatic."

"Probably. But I want to get this proposal right."

Her blue eyes widen. "Are you proposing right now?"

"Yes." I get down on my knees and then carefully pull off my shirt. There's plastic wrap clinging to the new ink on my chest. Words right there over my heart.

"That's gonna itch something terrible when that chest hair grows back," she says.

"You're worth it," I tell her.

She leans forward to read the words now inked into my skin. Then she looks up at me, tears swim in her eyes.

"Did you actually get the chorus to Love Story tattooed on your chest?"

"I did. Taylor Swift version, right? Not Shakespeare. That's us."

That earns me a huge smile. "Yeah, Romeo, that's us."

I pull the ring out of my pocket and hold it up to her. "Marry me?"

"YES!" She leans forward to kiss me, and the frosting pie sort of squishes between us.

"Oh, and we got the house."

"I love you," she says.

"Yeah, Juliette, I love you too."

***

I hope you loved Cruz and Juliette's story. Please consider **leaving me a review**.

Read the other books in the Dog Tags series:

Jack of Hearts

Fools Rush Flynn

Quid Pro Beau

Love 'em or Liam

Happily Evan After

Ready, Willing and Abel

Romero and Juliette

Grab **Redeem My Heart** if you want to see where Great Dane's Dog Sanctuary started.

Keep scrolling for an excerpt from another age-gap book from Saddle Creek, TX, **Awaken My Heart**

thank you for reading!

Join my newsletter for bonus epilogues, deleted scenes and a FREE BOOK.

join me!

COME JOIN my **VIP Reader Group on Facebook** where I do sneak peeks, answer questions and keep you up to date with everyone going on in Kat Baxter land.

excerpt from awaken my heart

BRAM

There are times when a man wants more than a cold beer to get him through the night. Times when even the comfort of a good conversation isn't enough to settle the restless parts of a man's soul.

The restless parts that want to stir up trouble, pick a fight, punch something, drive too fast and howl into the wind.

I work hard to bury those unruly parts of myself. I'm a grown-ass man, with four grown kids and grandkids. I'm a damn pillar of the community, for fuck's sake.

I'm too old and too set in my ways to give in to any of those urges.

Despite that, there's something in the air tonight that has me drinking my beer too quickly and my mind drifting from the conversation. I force my attention back to Graham, my best friend for forty years and the man currently seated across the high top from me.

"At least now your son has an option for a general practitioner instead of continuing to see me," Graham says. "He makes my other patients nervous."

I chuckle thinking about Garrett still trying to go to his pediatrician like he's not a fully grown adult. "Felicity is whipping him into shape."

Graham pops me on the back. "How does it feel to have all four of your kids engaged or married off? You're done now."

That's what everyone keeps telling me. I raised my kids and now I'm done. But I don't know what the fuck that means for my future. Which must be why I'm feeling this soul deep restlessness.

Because this was not the way it was supposed to go. She's been gone for more than fifteen years now; I should be used to the new normal. But I'm struggling. I was Lisa's husband and then I was our kids' dad. Now I'm really neither of those things and I'm not quite sure what I should do with myself.

Grady, my oldest, and our crew keep our family ranch running smoothly. He barely needs me around anymore. And there's only so many tomatoes a man can raise. I don't even like tomatoes. But no one would know that from walking past my back yard. It's a veritable tomato plantation out there.

Graham is regaling me with funny stories of what he pulled out of toddlers' noses this week when the front door to Ace's opens. I've got my burger halfway to my mouth, and then she walks in.

The first thing I notice is that she's new to Saddle Creek. I don't know if she's passing through or a new resident, but I know that I don't know her. And I know everyone.

And then I notice everything else about her, and it's like an assault to my senses. Her body is wrapped in one of those wrap-around dresses. It's bright pink with tiny flowers scattered across the fabric. She's plump and curvy in the very best way. The dress hugs her big tits, showing off a mouthwatering amount of cleavage. Her waist dips in just enough to highlight how thick and wide her hips are. Hips you can grab onto; leave bruised fingerprints on while fucking her from behind.

Her long brown hair falls around her shoulders, framing the most beautiful face I've ever laid eyes on.

No, that can't be right.

I mean she's objectively pretty, but the *prettiest*?

Somehow our eyes meet and that sugar sweet smile she has falters as our gazes lock.

Graham waves a napkin in front of me. "Hey, you're drooling on the bar, man."

I tear my eyes off of her and glare at my friend. "What are you rambling about?"

"Only that the eye fucking is making you drool."

I rip the napkin out of his hand and like a damned fool, I wipe my chin.

Graham bellows a laugh beside me.

"Fuck you," I mutter.

"Invite her over," Graham says.

"What for?"

"Uh, to meet her? You obviously think she's pretty."

"She is pretty. Objectively speaking," I snap.

Graham smiles and it just irritates me more. "Okay, we agree, she's pretty. Which is why you should meet her."

"I don't need to meet her. She's young enough to be my daughter. Doesn't look a day older than Daphne."

"Pretty sure you're wrong about that, but it doesn't matter. Age is just a number. It's time for you to get off the bench and get back on the field."

"Nice try, coach, but I'm not in this game."

"Right. Because you're so old. And she's young enough to be your daughter. Whatever." Graham points a French fry at me. "For the record, if you and Lisa had started having kids any earlier, you could be my dad too."

"Shut the fuck up," I grumble. But my eyes are on that woman again. The way she gifts everyone around her with that blinding smile. I want her to shine it at me. Just once.

"Just saying," Graham says. "You don't have to be out of the game. You can jump back in any time you want."

"You gotta stop saying shit like that. You know I'm done with that sort of thing."

"Yep, one woman man and all that. But I'm pretty sure all those songs were about only having one woman at a time, not your lifelong limit. Plus, it doesn't seem like you're all that done, considering you haven't looked away from that one since she walked in."

"She's alone. I'm just worried about her being in a bar alone. It's dangerous."

"In Saddle Creek?" Graham snorts. Then the bastard does the unthinkable. He catches her eye and calls her over.

She saunters towards us, and my eyes eat her

up. She's not a snack. She's a whole goddamn meal and fuck me if I don't want to savor every morsel. My dick goes rock hard in my jeans, and I nearly get lightheaded with how swiftly the blood rushes to my groin. What the fuck is even happening right now?

"You're new," Graham says in his smooth, flirty voice.

"Are y'all the welcome wagon?" she asks, smiling widely at my friend.

He laughs. "We sure are, sugar."

I have never wanted to throat punch him more.

"I'm Graham, but most people around here just call me Doc since I'm the local pediatrician." Graham makes a big show of kissing her hand. Then he thumps a hand against my stomach. "This here is my buddy, Bram."

She looks over at me.

Her gaze catches mine, and that smile dies right on her lips. Probably because I'm scowling like a mean son of a bitch.

"Bram, interesting name." Then she's all grins and giggles again as she looks at Graham. "I'm Emily. I mean Emma and yes, I am new to town. Just moved here a while back."

"Well, it's nice to meet you Emily, I mean Emma," Graham says.

"It's not safe for a young, single woman to be at a bar alone like this," I rumble.

Her brow arches as she looks at me. "I'm pretty sure my virtue is safe. Besides, I'm not alone, I'm meeting a friend. I believe she just walked in. If you two will excuse me."

"Welcome to Saddle Creek, Emma," Graham says.

"Thank you, Doc." She winks at him.

And I have the irrational urge to stab my fork in his thigh.

"Oh, and Bram," she says my name all short and clipped. "I'm older than I look." Then she walks off.

Graham bellows out another laugh. "She handed you your ass," he wheezes.

"You're an asshole." Then I sit there and stare at my half-eaten burger, unsure if I should go home and tend to those fucking tomato plants or if I should stay here and make sure Emma is safe.

Read **Awaken My Heart**

about the author

USA Today Bestselling Author, Kat Baxter writes fast-paced, sweet & STEAMY romantic comedies. Readers have dubbed her "The Queen of Adorkable." and her books "laugh-out-loud funny," and "hot enough to melt your kindle." She lives in Texas with her family and a menagerie of animals. Kat is the pseudonym for a bestselling historical romance author.

What readers have said about Kat's books:

"Kat Baxter is my catnip!" ~ Goodreads review

"Whenever I need my sexy nerdy dirty talking romance fix, I know Kat Baxter has my back!" ~Goodreads review

"How does Kat Baxter make me fall in love with her characters in just 12 short chapters? It's coz she's a freaken magic weaver with her words!!" ~ Amazon review

"You'll instantly fall in love." ~Goodreads review

"Swoon. I could not get enough of this story and fell in love with both these characters!" ~Amazon review

"… the chemistry between them is instant and off the charts!" ~Amazon review

"… original, hot, and a hoot!" ~Amazon review

"DAMN it's hot." ~Amazon review

"… sweetness, heat and humor. By the time the story was over, my cheeks hurt from smiling so hard." ~Amazon review

"Such a very sweet and spicy story!" ~ Goodreads

"The connection between the characters felt real, and I liked the author's writing style." ~ Goodreads

Made in the USA
Coppell, TX
20 January 2026

68886385R00075